CHAOTICALLY BEAUTIFUL
BY J.M. WISE

Printed in the United States of America

ISBN: 9780578826646

Author: @j.m.wise

Book Cover: @ellehell

Book Art Illustrator: @sidraws_

Photography: @d.a.ehernandez

Editor: Lorena Mejia

First Edition, 2021

jmwisewriting@gmail.com

www.jmwisewriting.com

Publisher: J.M. Wise Writing

if you have suffered
an intense heartbreak
these pages are for you

Chaotically Beautiful

<u>written for one who i still love</u>

i met you and became
instantly fascinated
by your every move.
i began to wonder where you
had been my entire life.

soon after,
our love story initiated
and eventually became
as sweet as morning coffee.

until one day,
we mismatched
and became transparent
to one another.

like a camera with
a 50-millimeter lens
i caught a glimpse of you
and fell in love
with my field of view

Chaotically Beautiful

your love for me vanished
in the most beautiful way

i seem to never find
the love that i look for

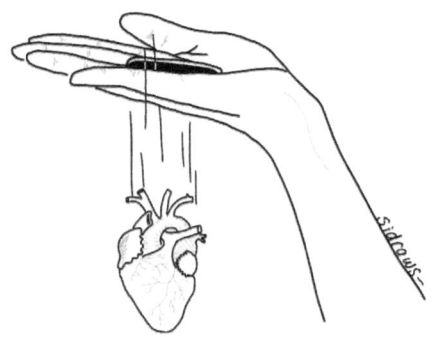

Chaotically Beautiful

in the depth of these words
is where you will find
the death of two worlds

J.M. Wise

we hurt to heal
and heal to hurt

Chaotically Beautiful

this heart of mine
gives more than
it receives

J.M. Wise

sun and moon

the sunlight brings out
the brightness in me

the moonlight brings out
the darkness in me

but you bring out
the best in me

Chaotically Beautiful

if only it was easy
to fall out of love

J.M. Wise

i see the beauty
of the sea
in your eyes

Chaotically Beautiful

and just like that
you appeared in my life
and just like that
you were gone from my life

J.M. Wise

a chaotic beauty like yours
causes the atomic isotopes
in my human body
to radiate the energetic radiation
that yields the intensity of my soul

Chaotically Beautiful

i hope your new match
lights up your world
the way i never did

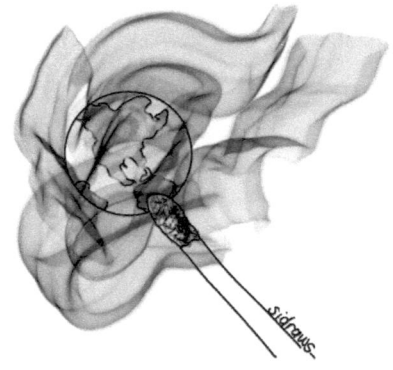

J.M. Wise

<u>love?</u>

someone once asked me,

if my love is meant for one soul
to cherish at the end of it all
then why must life present me
with more than one lover?

i responded,

i would say because
love is limitless.

life teaches some of us
that the love we shared
with our past lovers
and the lessons
we learned from them
occur so that we can finally meet
the soul who is meant for us.

Chaotically Beautiful

you loved me
when it was too late

J.M. Wise

i love too quickly and too easily
only to break my own heart

Chaotically Beautiful

i hope these rhymes of mine
remind you of why
you failed to be mine

J.M. Wise

my idea of love
consisted of a forever
but your inconsistency
never let us be a forever

Chaotically Beautiful

you are everything
that i ever looked for
and i am everything
that you never looked for

J.M. Wise

the aroma of your perfume
beautifully blooms
as it sets my love for you in fumes

Chaotically Beautiful

my body is ruled
by this mind of mine
but one night when
i was half wasted
my body was not ruled
by this mind of mine
it was forcibly ruled
by a man who thought
it was okay to rule
what is mine

- *she said*

J.M. Wise

even the sun envies
the way you shine

Chaotically Beautiful

you taught me love
but you also
taught me heartbreak

space and time
brought us together
only to separate us

Chaotically Beautiful

why would you ever chase after somebody
who walked away from you?
better yet, ran away from you?

somebody who sees your entire worth
will never leave you but instead
will make you feel loved and appreciated
without you asking for it.

J.M. Wise

i made you a mixtape full of songs
because i made a mistake full of wrongs

Chaotically Beautiful

i have never been able
to right my wrongs
that is why i write my wrongs

sun and moon II

her beauty splatters across the sky

in the day
she manifests yellow arrays
of sun rays that complement
the ocean of blue particles along
with pleasantly intoxicating clouds

in the night
she manifests the light of the moon
with the stars as glittery decorations
that prevail and exhibit her celestial beauty

Chaotically Beautiful

you are the beautiful soul
that is trapped in thoughts

even though
you forgot about me
i do not think
i could ever
forget about you

Chaotically Beautiful

i hurt others
when i am hurt
and when i am not hurt

i guess my heart
never fully heals
from being hurt

J.M. Wise

Chaotically Beautiful

you would never be able to comprehend
the love that i have for you
because a heart like yours
was made to manifest heartbreaks

J.M. Wise

i have spent years
trying to forget you

Chaotically Beautiful

<u>words i wish you never told me</u>

how about we go
our separate ways
and forget about
our old ways?

that is the only way
you will save yourself
from getting your heart
broken by me

J.M. Wise

the mirror's reflection reminds me that
life is full of ups and downs

the mirror's reflection reminds me that
those eyes that stare
right back at me have
seen it all and defeated it all

Chaotically Beautiful

you were bad for me
but i always yearn to attract
what is never good for me

J.M. Wise

i see you everywhere
as if i was stuck
in a world of mirrors
that reflect the image of you

Chaotically Beautiful

the coldness of your hand
touched the warmth of my chest
and fired up the coldness in my heart

J.M. Wise

we are all a little broken
in our own beautiful ways

Chaotically Beautiful

after our relationship perished
i wanted you more than ever

i felt the need to scream
out your name to the world
until the world around me
finally broke into pieces
the way you broke me into pieces

J.M. Wise

my love experiences
conceived a chaotically beautiful
rollercoaster of sentiments
that haunt me to this day

Chaotically Beautiful

your nude body
was a new body
to my world
of nobody

nobody
disembodied
me the way
your body did

J.M. Wise

this world of mine
collided with yours
and marked the ending
of our little universe

Chaotically Beautiful

i find it difficult
to love again

things i wish i told you

i was never good at relationships
but you made me want to try it out.

and even though we did not work out,
it was my mistake to try it out.

i should have known better.

Chaotically Beautiful

do not give the best of you
to those who do not see
the best in you

we met
our minds met
our souls met
our hands met
our lips met
our bodies met
but future us never met

Chaotically Beautiful

she is the type of woman
you will regret losing

you once told me i was not the one for you
but there i was readily available for you
with a bouquet of flowers just for you

it might have not meant anything to you
but being there for you
increased my optimism of being with you

all i wanted to do was worship your temple
as the tempo of our hearts
uncovered our deepest secrets

all i wanted to do was be the love of your life
show you where the sea meets the crest
in the sunken lands of the world
all i wanted to do was show you
that i do not fail to see the beauty
in you unlike the rest

and do it all over again
until we both sink deep underneath
the lands of our own little world

Chaotically Beautiful

i wonder if you
have eyes for me
the way i have
eyes for thee

J.M. Wise

we melted into
the arms of one another
and all for what?
to spill ourselves
into the arms of another?
heartbreaking.

Chaotically Beautiful

i loved you in ways
you could never love me

J.M. Wise

i am in that stage of my life
where i never make it
through talking stages

Chaotically Beautiful

no matter what i do
no matter where i go
it seems like i could never
let you go

J.M. Wise

you meant the world to me
so i took your hand and guided you
through my world
through my body
only for you to leave my world
and leave me as if i was a nobody

-she said

Chaotically Beautiful

you want to know
what is beautiful?
chaotically falling in love
with a person and infinitely
staying together

J.M. Wise

the anatomic and atomic
attraction that our bodies
possess for one another
magically unify us as one

Chaotically Beautiful

i was in love with you
unlike you who was in love
with the thought of being in love

J.M. Wise

beauty is all around you
just as beauty is within you

nothing burns more than
the old flame you still think about

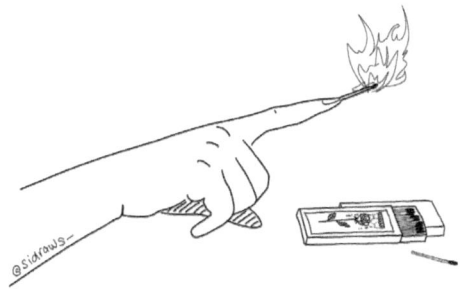

J.M. Wise

we are imperfect
yet we expect to be perfect

Chaotically Beautiful

sometimes i think
i have found the one.
we talk for a while
vibe for a while
hang out for a while
every once in a while
until one day one of us
stops replying as often
stops checking up as often
until one day one of us
stops talking to one another.
it is a vicious cycle that
my love life cannot seem to escape.

J.M. Wise

you were the home
that i never had

Chaotically Beautiful

you want to know
what is heartbreaking?
chaotically falling in love
with a beautiful soul
just to break apart in the end

here i am
sitting in the darkness
of my room
wondering why your heart
ran out of room
wondering why i let you
get the best of me
when you never let me
give you the best of me

Chaotically Beautiful

my mind loves to remember
those who forgot about me

J.M. Wise

a mind like mine
does not mind
loving a mind like yours

Chaotically Beautiful

love never lies.
so, when you said
you loved me
was that a lie
to uplift my life?

J.M. Wise

love twists tongues
the way tongues twist words

Chaotically Beautiful

the autumn leaves fall
as my heart leaves it all behind

J.M. Wise

i was afraid of losing you
when i should have been
afraid of losing myself

Chaotically Beautiful

sweetheart
that sweet heart
that your body possesses
undeniably possesses
what my sweet heart
desires to be possessed by

J.M. Wise

why be with someone unworthy
who makes your life difficult?
life is already as difficult as it is

truthfully, people are difficult
and that makes love even more difficult

be with someone
who makes your life easier
and if you can't seem to find them
wait for them to find you
because love will always find you
when you least expect it

Chaotically Beautiful

i knew i was not good enough for you
i knew you were not good for me
yet i was with you
in the hope of eventually
being good enough for you

J.M. Wise

walking away is difficult
but you must walk away
no matter how attached you are
to them because having them in your life
will never make your life less difficult.

once you realize that you are capable
of breaking yourself away
from those chains
you will be the happy individual
that you deserve to be.

Chaotically Beautiful

just as the Fall leaves
i fall colorless
and just as the Fall leaves
i grow again

J.M. Wise

one day
you will meet someone
you will fall in love with them
they will fall in love with you
and it will not be perfect
but it will be enough

Chaotically Beautiful

it is heartbreaking to see you
in love with someone else

J.M. Wise

my gullible brain believed
every word that came out
of your mouth and that was
my biggest mistake

-she said

Chaotically Beautiful

i dream of being
the person you
dream of being with

as i look up at the cosmos
i seek the answers to the questions
that constantly haunt me

as i look up at the cosmos
i free myself as my eyes freeze
the way masses of ice freeze

as i look up at the cosmos
i spin around in circles
realizing that i will probably never
get the answers to the questions
that constantly haunt me

Chaotically Beautiful

it has been so long
since you have been
long gone

J.M. Wise

you are beautifully cinematic
and i am just the protagonist
who happens to be
a part of my favorite movie

Chaotically Beautiful

my love for you is
chaotically beautiful

J.M. Wise

i needed you
but you needed me
more than i needed you

in the end, i realized that
we both needed ourselves
more than we needed each other

Chaotically Beautiful

i fully lost myself
within your love
whilst you were
full of lust and not of love

J.M. Wise

my soft heart still has
a soft spot for you

Chaotically Beautiful

i just want you to understand
that this life is beautiful and chaotic
and most of the time
you will fall somewhere in between both

whenever you are feeling chaotic
embrace the beauty within you
and whenever you are feeling beautiful
embrace the chaos within you

J.M. Wise

my nights became lonelier
after you left

missing them is no excuse
to hold yourself back
from moving on

J.M. Wise

in my fantasies is where
i am never the last option
but in reality
being the last option
is all i ever am

Chaotically Beautiful

i know how to love
but i do not know how to forget

J.M. Wise

her pretty face deserves
to display a pretty smile

Chaotically Beautiful

i love for the looks
and never look
for beauty in the mind.
that is why you must not
be like me who leads the blind.

J.M. Wise

our worlds collided
to create a kaleidoscope
of beautiful images

the sun and moon III

you exhibit your beauty
the way the sun and moon do

J.M. Wise

even after having
a broken heart
this broken vision
of mine still sees
the best of you

Chaotically Beautiful

i was wrong for loving you
and you were wrong
for not loving me

J.M. Wise

the thought
of you
drowns me

Chaotically Beautiful

sometimes it feels like
we met lifetimes ago.
sometimes i cannot even process
the fact that we were once together.

that first time we met
those times we meant
to give each other our all.

those moments feel surreal yet so real.
at times i just want to go back in time
not to just be with you again
but to be in love with you again

but then i remember
how we found happiness elsewhere.

you forgave me
and that is the least you ever did.

i still have not been able to forget you
but that is because everything you ever did
meant the world to me.

J.M. Wise

never forget that
you are chaotically beautiful
and i am beautifully chaotic
for you